To ████████
From Your Friend
At
Reading Connection

Cara

Secret in the Stable

Secret in the Stable

SCHOLASTIC INC.

New York   Toronto   London   Auckland   Sydney
Mexico City   New Delhi   Hong Kong   Buenos Aires

ISBN 10: 0-545-02924-4
ISBN 13: 978-0-545-02924-7

12 11 10 9 8 7 6 5 4 3 2 1   8 9 10 11 12 13/0

Printed in China
First printing, September 2008

The Only Hearts Girls™ formed the Only Hearts Club® in a bond of true friendship. They are a fun-loving bunch of friends who are always there for one another. They laugh, share secrets, and have the greatest adventures together. Most important, they encourage one another to listen to their hearts and to do the right thing.

*I*t was a big day for Olivia Hope. Not only was she performing in the Regional Equestrian Championship at Windy Way Stables, but also her family and friends were there to watch her compete.

Olivia loved everything about horses. In fact, the Windy Way Stables was almost like a second home to Olivia because she spent so much time there. She loved riding and grooming Missy, the golden horse with the long, flowing mane.

Secret in the Stable

Olivia did a final check to make sure Missy's saddle was on properly. Then she put on her riding jacket and secured her helmet.

"Are you nervous?" asked her friend, Anna Sophia, as her puppy, Bubulina, sat near her.

Olivia shook her head. "Nope. Just excited!" she replied. "I'm glad you're all here," she added, looking at her best friends.

"We wouldn't miss it!" insisted Taylor Angelique, as she held her beagle, Patches.

Olivia knew Taylor was right. Olivia felt lucky to be part of the Only Hearts Club—eight friends who had formed a club with a promise to listen to their hearts and do the right thing.

Secret in the Stable

Outside a nearby stall, Lily Rose and her puppy, Cupcake, cooed over Bitsy, Missy's baby. The young foal looked like a pint-sized version of her mother.

"You are so adorable," Lily said, gently petting the foal's nose.

Just then, Olivia's trainer, Ms. Anderson, came into the stable. She gave Olivia some last-minute reminders and then announced that it was time to go. The girls wished Olivia good luck as she and Missy headed out. Then the friends and their dogs walked to the stands.

"This is so cool," said Briana Joy as she and her dog, Longfellow, took their seats next to Olivia's parents and their yellow Labrador Retreiver, Sniff.

"I'll bet Olivia gets the blue ribbon," Karina Grace said as she petted her Dalmatian, Dotcom.

Olivia's mother smiled at the girls. She was happy Olivia had such supportive friends.

Secret in the Stable

But one girl was still back at the stables.

"I'll be there in a minute," Lily had told the others. She wanted to spend a little more time with Bitsy.

Suddenly Lily had an idea: Wouldn't it be fun to bring Bitsy out to watch her mommy, Missy, perform in the show? Lily knew that it could be dangerous to do anything that could distract a horse in the ring, so she had to be extra careful bringing Bitsy near Missy. She promised herself that they wouldn't get too close. Quickly, Lily led Bitsy out of her stall and put a lead line on her. The pair started walking out toward the ring.

Secret in the Stable

Soon it was Olivia's turn, and she entered the ring with a big smile on her face. She and Missy needed to complete a course that included several jumps.

"This is it," she whispered to her horse. "This is what we've practiced so hard for. Let's go!" Olivia pressed her heels into Missy's side, and the horse cantered forward.

First was a single fence. Olivia and Missy easily sailed over it. As Missy approached the next jump, Olivia leaned forward in the saddle, just as she had practiced. She concentrated on keeping her eyes forward and her back straight, as Missy took to the air. They cleared the rails and landed safely on the other side. A cheer broke out in the crowd. Olivia was sure she could hear her friends yelling the loudest, but she tried to stay focused.

Secret in the Stable

One jump after another, Olivia and Missy performed flawlessly.

"Okay, girl, just one more to go," Olivia whispered as they prepared for the final jump.

As Missy cantered forward, disaster struck. Missy spotted her baby, Bitsy, approaching the ring with Lily. Missy became distracted and swerved to the right. The sudden movement caught Olivia completely off guard, and she fell from the horse!

The audience gasped and stood up. Was Olivia okay? A fellow rider carefully took Missy's reins to lead her away from Olivia as Ms. Anderson and Olivia's parents rushed into the ring to help her. Olivia was lucky; she was only slightly bruised. More than anything else, she was embarrassed and scared by the fall. That had never happened before. *What would make Missy do that?* Olivia wondered. *Did I do something wrong?*

Secret in the Stable

In truth, Olivia hadn't done anything wrong. Lily had. She shouldn't even have brought Bitsy out of the stables. Lily watched in horror as Olivia fell from her horse. She quickly turned Bitsy around and raced back to the stables.

"I hope no one saw us," Lily said to Bitsy in a desperate voice.

Once Lily joined her friends at the ring, it was clear that none of them had seen her and Bitsy. She knew that if she didn't say anything, no one would ever know that it was Lily's fault that Missy had thrown Olivia. Lily sighed with relief.

"I still can't believe it," said Hannah Faith as the friends headed toward the stables to meet up with Olivia.

"Me either," Kayla Rae agreed. "I mean, Olivia is a *great* rider. No one practices more than her."

Secret in the Stable

Meanwhile, in the stables, Ms. Anderson spoke to Olivia.

"You must maintain your focus all the way until the end of the course," Ms. Anderson said. It was clear that the trainer was disappointed.

Olivia just nodded silently. She felt disappointed, too.

Once Ms. Anderson left, Olivia couldn't hold back her tears any longer. It wasn't the fact that she hadn't won that bothered her. Instead, she felt embarrassed to have fallen in front of her friends and family.

Just then, her friends walked up to her in the stable and gave her great big hugs. Olivia explained that she didn't know what went wrong.

Lily began to feel a knot growing in her stomach and uneasiness in her heart. She felt terrible for Olivia, but Lily was afraid she'd get into trouble if she told the truth. Lily didn't know what to do.

Secret in the Stable

Over the next few days, it was clear that Olivia was still shaken up by her fall. "I'm scared to get back on Missy," she revealed to her friends. "What if I do something wrong and fall again?"

Her friends did their best to reassure Olivia, but it wasn't working. Worst of all, Olivia never seemed to smile anymore.

"I have an idea," Karina said, once Olivia had gone home.

Briana smiled. "You *always* have an idea," she teased.

"And they're usually good," Karina replied with a grin. "How about we pool our baby-sitting money and buy Olivia a special gift to remind her how much she loves horses and how good she is at riding?"

"That's awesome!" said Taylor. "It might be just what Olivia needs to get back in the saddle."

The other girls agreed. They were so excited that they didn't notice that Lily was strangely silent.

Secret in the Stable

After school the next day, the girls went to the mall to buy the special gift for Olivia. All the way there, Lily felt terrible. She kept going over her dilemma in her head. She could admit the truth and tell Olivia that it was not her or Missy's fault. But then everyone might be mad at her. Or she could just say nothing. Because no one actually had seen her and Bitsy, no one would ever know Lily was at fault. All Lily really had to do was keep quiet, and maybe the whole situation would go away. But it just seemed to be getting worse. She never expected that what she had done with Bitsy would make Olivia fearful of riding.

All that week, Lily could think of nothing else. She avoided the other girls for a few days as her heart grew heavy with guilt. Maybe she should avoid the issue, stay silent, and hope everyone just forgot about it over time, she thought to herself. But when it was time to give Olivia the gift, Lily knew that she *had* to show up.

Secret in the Stable

Olivia was surprised to see all her friends standing on her front porch. She invited them in, and they went up to her bedroom.

"I'm always happy to see you guys, but what are you doing here?" asked Olivia.

Hannah stood up. "As your best friends in the world, we want to see you ride again."

"We know you're scared," said Kayla. "So we all pitched in and bought you something special to remind you how much you love riding and how good a rider you are."

"And to remind you to listen to your heart—even when it's scary to," added Taylor.

Olivia was overcome with emotion. She carefully unwrapped the gift. It was a beautiful necklace with a charm of a mommy and baby horse — just like Missy and Bitsy! "I couldn't ask for better friends!" she gushed.

Lily cringed. She felt like an imposter.

Secret in the Stable

Lily felt like her heart was breaking. She didn't know how much longer she could keep up the lie. She wanted to see Olivia riding again, see her smiling again. As she walked home, Lily remembered the pledge she had made to the Only Hearts Club. Suddenly she knew she had to do the most difficult thing: She had to listen to her heart and do the right thing. She had to tell the truth.

The following day, the Only Hearts Girls had agreed to meet up at the stables for Olivia's first riding lesson since the fall. Before the lesson began, Lily asked for everyone's attention.

"I have to tell you all something important about Olivia's fall," she said. "Okay, here goes: Olivia, you and Missy did nothing wrong. The fall was all my fault."

Puzzled and confused, everyone looked at Lily.

Lily took a deep breath and continued. "I thought it would be nice for Bitsy to see her mommy compete, so I brought her out from the stable. I thought we were far enough away from the ring, but Missy saw Bitsy and moved toward her right before the last jump. That's what made you fall off."

Olivia's eyes grew wide as the others exchanged glances.

"I never meant to do anything that might hurt you," Lily told Olivia. "Having you believe you did something wrong was worse than anything." Then she walked up to Olivia and pointed to the charm around her neck. "You don't need a charm to tell you that you're a great rider. *I'm* the one who messed everything up, not you."

Secret in the Stable

A huge feeling of relief washed over Olivia. She was thrilled that it wasn't her fault that she fell from her horse. And she knew her parents and her trainer would be glad to know the truth as well.

Even though Lily thought she did the right thing by confessing, she suddenly felt like an outsider. She slowly started walking away.

Suddenly, Olivia shouted Lily's name. Lily winced, then slowly turned around, afraid of the anger that she was certain was coming. She walked hesitantly back to the group.

Secret in the Stable

"Why did you wait so long to tell the truth?" Olivia asked Lily.

Lily looked at the ground. "I'm sorry I didn't tell you sooner. I was afraid everyone would be mad at me. I understand if you don't want to be my friend anymore," Lily said in a quiet voice.

"Not be your friend?" repeated Olivia. "But we're all members of the Only Hearts Club. We're best friends forever. Right, guys?" She looked at the others who nodded in agreement.

"Really?" Lily asked, surprised that she was forgiven.

"Really," Olivia reassured her. "I'm sure a lot of people would never have admitted the truth. But you did, and that helped me a lot. You made a mistake, but you admitted the truth and were a good friend. That really means something."

Lily hugged Olivia tightly. "Sorry again," Lily said. "And thank you for understanding and being a good friend, too."

Secret in the Stable

At that moment, Ms. Anderson approached Olivia.

"Do you feel ready to go for a ride on Missy?" the trainer asked. "Just a nice and easy one."

Olivia looked up at her trainer and then at the girls. She saw the encouraging faces of her best friends. Would she be able to return to riding without being scared?

"You can do it!" Briana declared.

"Yeah!" agreed Karina. "And we'll be right here watching the whole time."

Olivia's eyes twinkled. "I have a better idea . . ."

Secret in the Stable

Laughter and good cheer radiated from the girls as they rode horses along the trail. Olivia had decided that her first time back in the saddle would be easier if her friends were right by her side. The friends had readily agreed.

As Lily felt the breeze blow back her hair, she was glad she had listened to her heart and had friends who were understanding and forgiving.

Another happy rider was Olivia. For the first time since the fall, she was wearing the best accessory. . . a smile.

About the Only Hearts Club

Only Hearts Club® is a fashion doll brand that delivers a positive image and message to girls. The soft, poseable dolls feature amazing detail, and look and dress like real girls, in age-appropriate fashions. The brand's message, delivered through a series of Only Hearts Club books, is to "listen to your heart and do the right thing." This image and message are unique.

As detailed in their books, and through available playsets, outfits, and accessories, the Only Hearts Girls™ share the interests and experiences of real girls. They love horses and enjoy visiting the stable and horseback riding as part of the Horse & Pony Club™.

The Only Hearts Girls™ also have lots of fun at sleepovers and babysitting their younger siblings, the Only Hearts Li'l Kids™.

The other interests of the members of the Only Hearts Club® include dancing, ballet, sports such as soccer, arts and crafts, cooking and baking, and exploring the outdoors.

They are especially fond of animals, such as the Only Hearts Pets™, and love caring for them, feeding them, and playing with them.

Girls and parents love the Only Hearts Club:

"Thank you for making such wonderful dolls that are a better alternative and teach better values to girls."

"It's nice that someone is making dolls that are so much like me."

"Thank you for making dolls that are young and sweet, just like my children."

"I love, love, LOVE your dolls! Your books are wonderful too!"

Available at TARGET stores and specialty toy and gift stores nationwide.

www.OnlyHeartsClub.com